This book
belongs to -
....

ISBN 0 86163 046 7

© Award Publications Limited
Spring House, Spring Place
London NW5, England

Fifth edition 1981

Printed in Hungary

NURSERY STORIES

WRITTEN & ILLUSTRATED
BY
RENE CLOKE

AWARD PUBLICATIONS—LONDON

THE RED UMBRELLA

"I think I will have a picnic by the river," said Ricky Rabbit.

He looked out of the window; the sun was shining but there were some big clouds in the sky.

"Perhaps I had better take my umbrella," he said, "it might rain and I <u>don't</u> like getting wet."

He put on his scarf, packed a flask of tea and a bag of biscuits, then he picked a big lettuce from the garden.

On the way to the river he called at the baker's shop and bought some currant buns and jam tarts.

"My little Dan and Daisy went down to the river this morning," said Mr Harvest Mouse, the baker, "and they haven't come home yet. Look out for them, will you?"

"I will," answered Ricky. "Now, tell me, do you think it will rain?"

"Oh, no!" laughed Mr Harvest Mouse, "it's a lovely day!"

"Rather a pity I brought my umbrella," thought Ricky.

The first person he met as he walked through the woods to the river was Hopscotch, the frog.

Hopscotch was feeling very cross.

"I want to take home some blackberries," he grumbled, "but they are all growing so high up that I can't reach them, fine hopper though I am."

Ricky hooked his umbrella over a branch and pulled it down.

"Oh, thank you!" cried Hopscotch, as he filled his cans, "that's splendid. I shall have enough to make bramble jelly and I will give you a pot to put in your store cupboard."

"That's very kind of you," said Ricky, "I'm fond of bramble jelly."

Ricky hummed a little tune as he walked on through the woods but he had rather a fright when he saw old Foxy taking a short cut to his den over the hill. Ricky and Foxy were not good friends and Foxy had a very hungry look in his eyes today.

"I mustn't let him see me," said Ricky and he looked around for a good hiding place.

Some big red toadstools were growing nearby, so Ricky put up his umbrella and popped underneath it.

Old Foxy thought that the red umbrella was another toadstool and went on his way without noticing the little rabbit.

"That was lucky," whispered Ricky.

He skipped along by the river looking for a comfortable place to have his tea and talking to some of the birds and animals he met.

Then he heard a little cry –

"Help! help!"

"Who is that?" called Ricky looking across the water.

There, on the grassy island in the middle of the river, Ricky saw Dan and Daisy, the two little harvest mice.

"We rowed our boat up the river and landed on this island," cried Dan.

"But the boat drifted away," sobbed Daisy, "and we can't get back."

"This looks like another job for my umbrella," decided Ricky.

He opened the big umbrella and floated it on the water, then he stepped inside and paddled out to the island.

"Oh, Ricky, you are clever," cried Dan, as he and Daisy scrambled in and Ricky paddled the umbrella back to the bank.

"Your umbrella makes a lovely boat," said Daisy.

"You must be hungry," said Ricky, when they were all safely ashore, "there's plenty in my basket for you both to share."

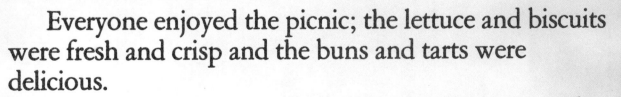

Everyone enjoyed the picnic; the lettuce and biscuits were fresh and crisp and the buns and tarts were delicious.

"Although it didn't rain," said Ricky, "it's very lucky that I took my umbrella."

BOB-A-CAT

Bob-a-Cat helped himself to marmalade and said –
"I'm going shopping to-day."
"What are you going to buy?" asked Dickory.
"Ah," replied Bob-a-Cat, mysteriously, "that's a secret."
Dickory thought this sounded most exciting, especially as the next day was his birthday and he couldn't help wondering if the secret might be something for him.

He pretended not to be interested and just said –
"Don't eat all the marmalade, I haven't finished my toast."

After breakfast Bob-a-Cat took his purse from his drawer; he knew exactly how much he had – seventy-five pence, enough to buy a nice birthday present.

He popped his head round the kitchen door.
"I'm off, Dic," he called.

Dickory was reading a cookery book and waved his hand without looking up. Bob-a-Cat had made him a birthday cake but he thought he would make some jam tarts and buns as well for his birthday party tomorrow.

Bob-a-Cat tried to think of the best kind of birthday present for Dickory.
"He has a bat and ball and a bucket and spade, I must think of something quite new."
He crossed the river by the little bridge and thought about boats, but Dickory already had two.
He met Barbara Bunny riding her bicycle.
"I'd like to buy Dickory a bicycle," thought Bob-a-Cat, "but I'm afraid they cost more than seventy-five pence."

When he reached the market, he found that the stalls
were full of such wonderful things that he
was quite bewildered.

"I won't buy sweets or chocolates,"
he decided, "I might want to eat
them myself."

He saw some gay hats
on another stall.

"But I don't know
what size to get," said
Bob-a-Cat, "and a hat
that didn't fit would be a
silly sort of present."

The next stall was the best; there were garden
tools and watering-cans and little wheelbarrows,
red, green and blue.

"Dickory would like a wheelbarrow for the garden
better than anything," sighed Bob-a-Cat, "but, oh
dear, they're ninety pence and I've only seventy-five."

He wandered round the market looking at saucepans
and brushes and other unbirthday kind of things and, at
last, he went back to the stall with the wheelbarrows.

"Trying to make up your mind which colour to have?"
asked old Badger, the stall keeper.

"They're all beautiful," said Bob-a-Cat, "but I haven't got
ninety pence, have you – have you – just one that's cheaper?"

"Well, as a matter of fact, I have,"
said the stall keeper, "this one is a
bit scratched; I was going to
touch it up with some
red paint –

90ᴾ

– but I'll let you have it for seventy-five pence." "Oh, thank
you!" gasped Bob-a-Cat, "it's a lovely one!" He paid old
Badger and trundled off with the wheelbarrow.

When Bob-a-Cat got home he crept around to the back of the house and pushed the wheelbarrow into the garden shed.

He painted over the scratches with red paint and it looked as good as new, then he hid it behind a box and tip-toed along to the front door.

"Hullo," said Dickory, "did you get your secret?"

"Wait and see," laughed Bob-a-Cat. He wasn't carrying anything except his empty purse; it was all very exciting and mysterious.

Bob-a-Cat had a glass of milk for supper and Dickory had some cocoa; they ate two broken jam tarts which were not good enough for the party.

When Bob-a-Cat awoke the next morning, Dickory was still asleep.

"I'll put the wheelbarrow beside the breakfast table," whispered Bob-a-Cat as he hurried downstairs and out into the garden.

It was a beautiful morning, the sun was shining and the flowers were nodding in a very birthdayish kind of way.

Bob-a-Cat looked inside the shed – he looked behind the box – the wheelbarrow –

WASN'T THERE!

He peered here and there and everywhere, what could have happened to it?

"It's gone – it's gone!" he cried, running back to the house, "my wonderful secret present has gone!"

"What <u>is</u> the matter?" asked Dickory, "have you lost something?"

"It's your birthday present," sobbed Bob-a-Cat, "I hid it in the shed and now it's gone!"

Dickory helped him to search but, of course, he didn't know what to look for.

"It's big and red," said Bob-a-Cat, "but I can't tell you what it is because it's a secret."

"Hullo," called Mr Ottery, the postman, "I knocked at your door an hour ago but you must have been asleep.

I had so many letters and parcels for Dickory that I took a little wheelbarrow from your shed to put them in; you'll find them in the front porch."

Bob-a-Cat flew round the house and, there in the porch, was the wheelbarrow full of presents.

"It's the most wonderful secret present I've ever had!" gasped Dickory.

"Happy Birthday!" shouted Bob-a-Cat.

"Happy Birthday!" laughed the postman, "and don't oversleep next time!"

SILLY SQUIRRELS

Some squirrels are very silly; they can't see further than the end of their noses. If they could see as far as the end of their bushy tails they would be very wise indeed.

"Let's do something special for Christmas," said Bilberry.

"Let's not wash up," suggested Candytuft.

"That's a good idea," said Bilberry, "it's Christmas Eve tomorrow, we won't wash up for three days. Nothing could be more special than not washing up."

Bilberry and Candytuft had a lovely time on the next day; they hung paper chains and balloons all over the house and hung a garland of holly on the front door, they made a snowman and they went sliding on the pond.

They didn't wash up the breakfast dishes or the mid-morning drinks or the lunch; by the time they had finished tea there were stacks and stacks of plates and cups and saucers as well as knives and forks and spoons in the kitchen.

You wouldn't think that two squirrels could use so many dishes.

It was getting cold and dark so Bilberry took his lantern and they both looked out for the postman.

"Some letters and parcels for you both," cried Mr Rabbity, "and a telegram."

"Who can this be from?" said Bilberry as he tore it open. "EXPECT US BOTH FOR CHRISTMAS DAY LOVE UNCLE FUZZ AND AUNT BUSHY."

Bilberry and Candytuft were delighted. They went back to the kitchen, but, oh dear! There was the pile of dishes waiting to be washed and nothing clean for a Christmas Day party.

"This will take us all night," declared Candytuft seizing a bowl and turning the tap. But there was no water.

"The pipes have frozen," moaned Bilberry, "now what shall we do?"

"Get a bucket of snow and melt it on the fire," said Candytuft.

They were tired out by bedtime and Bilberry said he would rather go to bed without any supper than fetch more snow to wash up the plates afterwards.

The next morning they were both up early.

"Hurray!" cried Bilberry, "the thaw has come and the taps are running!"

Candytuft made some mince pies, Bilberry polished the spoons and forks and the table was set with the nice clean china just as Uncle Fuzz and Aunt Bushy drove up to the door.

"Merry Christmas!" called out Aunt Bushy, "I've brought you a Christmas cake for tea."

"Merry Christmas!" shouted Uncle Fuzz as he struggled to get a huge package from his car. "Here's a present that I think you'll find really useful!"

And what do you think it was?

A DISHWASHER